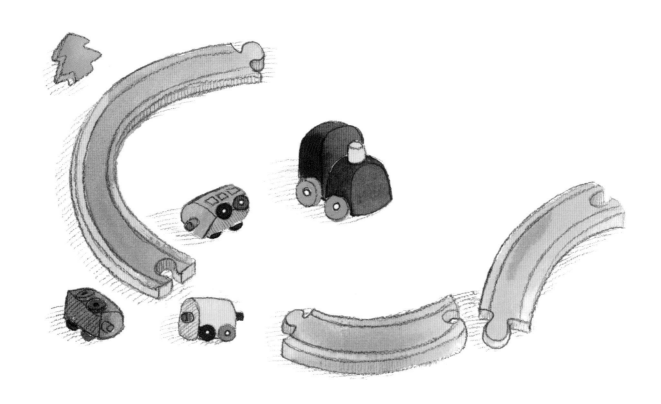

Written by David Bedford
Illustrated by Susie Poole

First published 2016 by Parragon Books, Ltd.
Copyright © 2018 Cottage Door Press, LLC
5005 Newport Drive, Rolling Meadows, Illinois 60008
All Rights Reserved

10 9 8 7 6 5 4 3 2

ISBN 978-1-68052-455-0

# You're a **BIG** Brother

PaRRagon.

You're going to be a big brother!
Hurray! How lucky are you?

Babies LOVE their big brothers

and all the smart things that they do.

Babies are funny and friendly,

but there are things a big brother
soon knows ...

Babies can SMELL ...

and pull hair as well ...

so watch out and hold onto your nose!

Babies make moms and dads busy—
they won't just be caring for you.

But now that you're a big brother,
it's fun sharing with somebody new.

Babies don't do much to start with,

so just quietly show them your toys.

They can't dance or sing,

but they like
to join in ...

by making a gurgling noise!

Babies learn lots from big brothers,
so teach them all you can do:

Share and
take care ...

be baby's best friend,

and they'll be amazing ...

just like YOU!

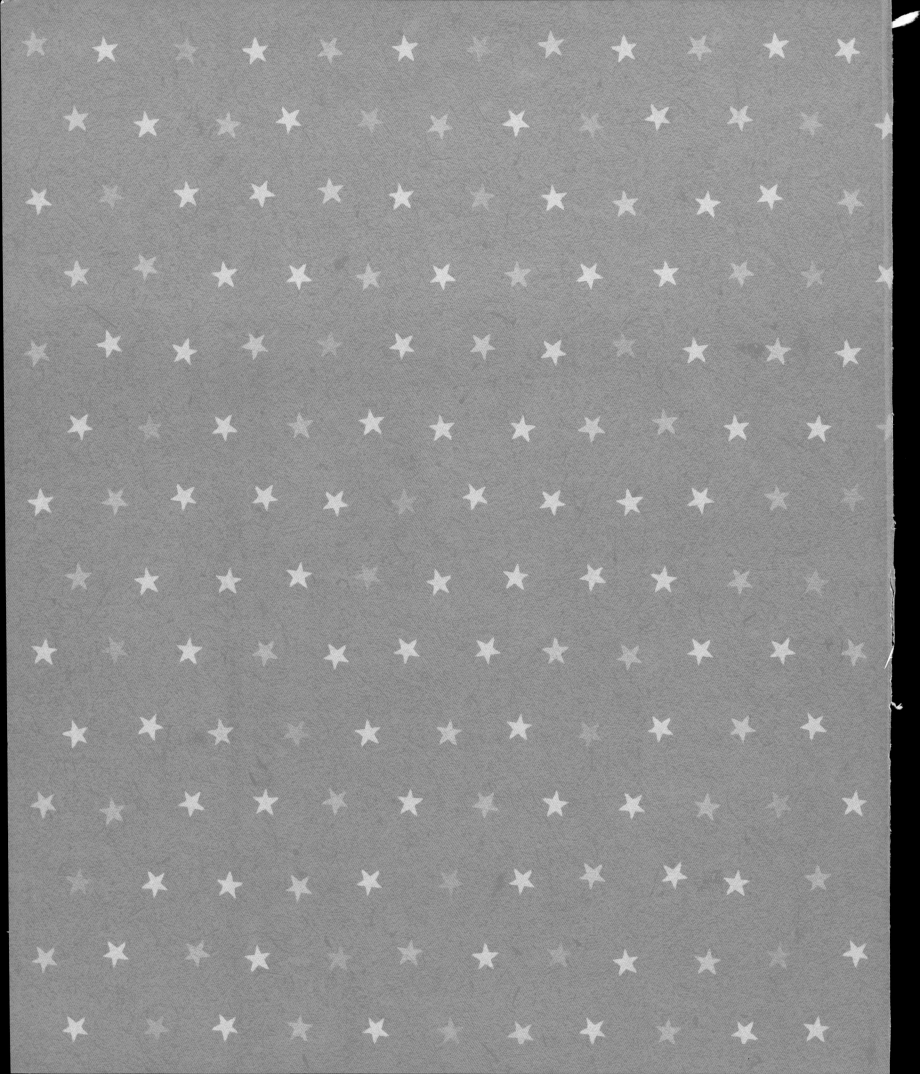